Ladybug Girl and Bingo

by David Soman and Jacky Davis

Dial Books for Young Readers
an imprint of Penguin Group (USA) Inc.

For Dimitri

DIAL BOOKS FOR YOUNG READERS
A division of Penguin Young Readers Group
Published by The Penguin Group
Penguin Group (USA) Inc., 375 Hudson Street, New York, NY 10014, U.S.A.
 Penguin Group (Canada), 90 Eglinton Avenue East, Suite 700, Toronto, Ontario, Canada M4P 2Y3 (a division of Pearson Penguin Canada Inc.)
Penguin Books Ltd, 80 Strand, London WC2R 0RL, England
Penguin Ireland, 25 St. Stephen's Green, Dublin 2, Ireland (a division of Penguin Books Ltd)
Penguin Group (Australia), 250 Camberwell Road, Camberwell, Victoria 3124, Australia (a division of Pearson Australia Group Pty Ltd)
Penguin Books India Pvt Ltd, 11 Community Centre, Panchsheel Park, New Delhi - 110 017, India
Penguin Group (NZ), 67 Apollo Drive, Rosedale, Auckland 0632, New Zealand (a division of Pearson New Zealand Ltd)
Penguin Books (South Africa) (Pty) Ltd, 24 Sturdee Avenue, Rosebank, Johannesburg 2196, South Africa
Penguin Books Ltd, Registered Offices: 80 Strand, London WC2R 0RL, England

Designed by Teresa Dikun and Jasmin Rubero
Text set in Old Claude LP Regular
Manufactured in China on acid-free paper

10 9 8 7 6 5 4 3 2

Library of Congress Cataloging-in-Publication Data
Soman, David.
Ladybug Girl and Bingo / by David Soman and Jacky Davis.
p.   cm.
Summary: Lulu, who likes to dress in a ladybug costume, goes camping with her parents, brother, and dog Bingo.
ISBN 978-0-8037-3582-8 (hardcover)
Special Markets ISBN 978-0-8037-4031-0 Not for resale
[1. Camping—Fiction. 2. Dogs—Fiction.] I. Davis, Jacky, date. II. Title.
PZ7.S696224Lag 2012
[E]—dc22
2011010013

This Imagination Library edition is published by Penguin Group (USA), a Pearson
company, exclusively for Dolly Parton's Imagination Library, a not-for-profit
program designed to inspire a love of reading and learning, sponsored in part by The Dolly-
wood Foundation. Penguin's trade editions of this work are available wherever books are sold.

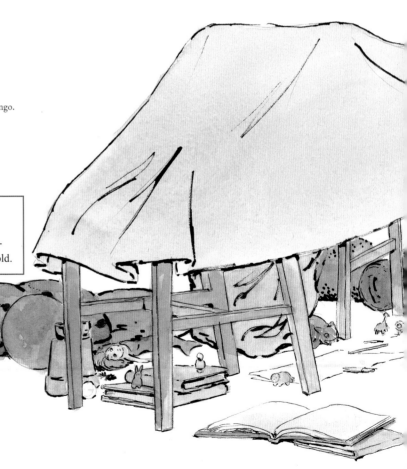

Ladybug Girl and Bingo

by David Soman and Jacky Davis

Dial Books for Young Readers
an imprint of Penguin Group (USA) Inc.

"This is where we should put the tent!" says Lulu.

She's excited to be camping, and to sleep in her new sleeping bag.

"Isn't this fun, Bingo? We're going to sleep outside!"

But Bingo isn't standing by her side like he usually does.

He's zigzagging all over the campsite,

Holding Bingo's leash extra-tight, she climbs to the top of the boulder.

From this high up, she can see the entire forest. She sees the Old Wizard Tree!

And then looking down she realizes she is standing on the Giant Turtle Rock! Ladybug Girl can even see their tent.

Ladybug Girl and Bingo
run breathlessly back to the campsite.

"Mama, Papa, guess what!?
We were searching for a lost unicorn, but then Bingo escaped into the woods,
and I chased him forever. And then when I found him, we were both
lost in the woods, but then Bingo helped me figure out where we were,
and we made it back—all by ourselves!"

"You weren't lost," says her brother. "You were right over there.
We could see your wings the whole time."
Ladybug Girl looks in the direction where they came from.
It is really far away; maybe her brother doesn't need glasses after all.

Later, after dinner, they toast marshmallows around the fire.
"Can you believe we're up so late, Bingo?" Lulu asks, staring at
the stars that cover the whole sky.

"Wow, there are even stars in the trees!"
Lulu says.

"Those aren't stars," her brother says,

"they're fireflies."

"Fireflies?"

"You should like them," he says.

"They're bugs that light up."

When it's time to go to sleep, Ladybug Girl wriggles
into her new sleeping bag with Bingo.
"I love you, Bingo," Lulu whispers.

It has been a long day, and Ladybug Girl

is a little bit sleepy, but tonight . . .

Firefly Girl is up!